Vampire Haters

Paul Blum

RISING STARS

nasen
Helping Everyone Achieve

NASEN House, 4/5 Amber Business Village, Amber Close,
Amington, Tamworth, Staffordshire, B77 4RP

Rising Stars UK Ltd.
7 Hatchers Mews, Bermondsey Street, London SE1 3GS
www.risingstars-uk.com

Published 2012

Cover design: Burville-Riley Partnership
Brighton photographs: iStock
Illustrations: Chris King for Illustration Ltd (characters and cover artwork)/
Abigail Daker (map) http://illustratedmaps.info
Text design and typesetting: Geoff Rayner
Publisher: Rebecca Law
Editorial manager: Sasha Morton Creative Project Management

British Library Cataloguing in Publication Data.
A CIP record for this book is available from the British Library.

ISBN: 978-0-85769-602-1

Printed and bound by CPI Group (UK) Ltd, Croydon, CR0 4YY

MIX
Paper from
responsible sources
FSC
www.fsc.org   FSC® C020471

Contents

Name:
John Logan

Age:
24

Hometown:
Manchester

Occupation:
Author of
supernatural
thrillers

Special skills:
Not yet known

profiles

Name:
Rose Petal

Age:
22

Hometown:
Brighton

Occupation:
Yoga teacher,
nightclub and
shop owner,
vampire hunter

Special skills:
Private investigator
specialising in
supernatural
crime

Location map

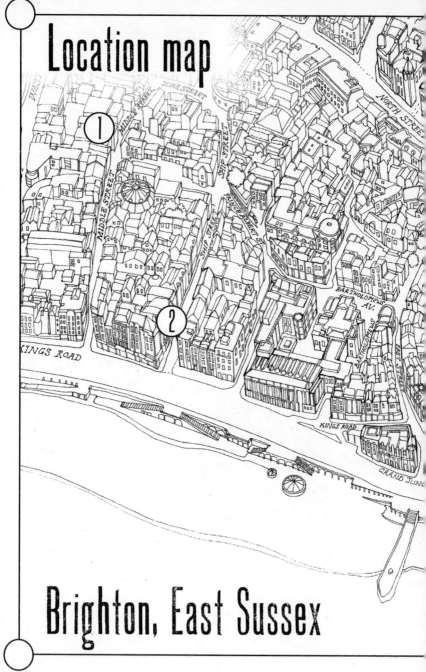

Brighton, East Sussex

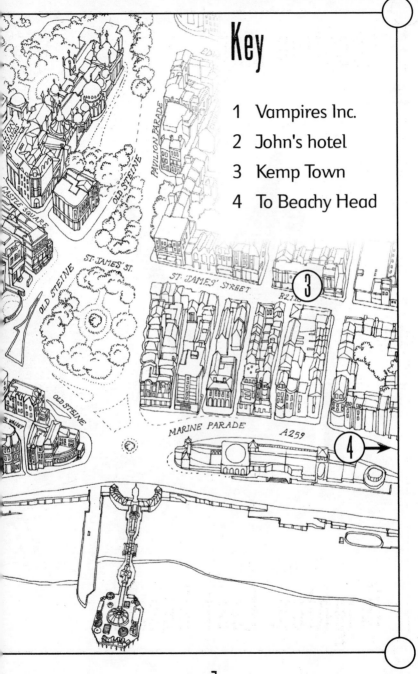

Key

1 Vampires Inc.
2 John's hotel
3 Kemp Town
4 To Beachy Head

Chapter 1

Vampires Inc. was one of the smallest nightclubs in Brighton, but it was jam-packed on Halloween. Inside there was a crowd of happy partygoers in Halloween costumes. Many of them were human and a good few were vampires. Brighton was a tolerant city and Vampires Inc. was the hottest place in town tonight.

Four new visitors to Vampires Inc. were Lomax and his buddies. Lomax was tall, blond and dressed in a Dracula costume. He turned a lot of heads. Tonight he was interested in making some more new friends – Tara and her boyfriend, Paul. Paul was a vampire and Tara was a human.

'Do you guys want to come to a party with us?' asked Lomax. 'We're going to see some friends in Hove. They're like us, they always enjoy meeting new people.'

'Sure,' said Tara. Lomax grabbed his costume Dracula cloak and grinned, showing his plastic fangs. 'Let's go!'

****

Lomax drove fast along the coast road towards Hove. Suddenly, he turned off into a small lane, heading into the countryside.

'Where are we going?' asked Paul.

'Just picking up another friend for the party,' said Lomax. 'Relax!'

But they just kept on driving down darker and darker lanes. Paul started to feel more worried. Finally, they stopped outside a brightly lit stable and Lomax turned off the engine.

'So, which one of you is the vampire?' asked Lomax. 'Both of you or just one?'

'What are you talking about?' said Tara. 'Is this where the party is?'

Lomax just smiled and looked at his friends. 'Now we're here the party can start. You see, me and my friends, we really hate vampires.'

'Vampires are scum,' said the woman. 'They don't deserve to go on living.'

11

'That's right,' grinned Lomax. 'And I'm going to make all of you undead bloodsuckers as dead as I can!'

Lomax and his friends pulled Paul and Tara out of the car. They dragged them towards the stable and pushed the door open. Inside was a beautiful white horse.

'You know the best test for a vampire?' asked Lomax. 'You get a white stallion to sniff them out. Who's going to take the first ride?'

Paul tried to break free and run but Lomax's gang was too strong. The men held him tightly while the woman pushed Tara against the wooden wall.

'Put him on first,' said Lomax, standing back. Two of his friends dragged Paul over to the horse. He couldn't escape. The horse panicked when it saw him and its eyes rolled back. It reared up on its hind legs and kicked Paul to the ground.

'That's one vampire identified,' said Lomax with a grin. 'Now test the girl!'

'Leave us alone,' Tara screamed. She stamped on the foot of the woman who was holding her. In shock, she let go of her victim for just long enough. Tara leapt onto the horse. 'I'll get help, Paul, hang on!' she shouted. Before they could stop her, Tara rode past them. She sobbed as she escaped into the night.

14

Chapter 2

The stable at Hill Top Farm was closed
off. Two police officers let Rose Petal
past as soon as they saw her, but they
stopped John Logan.

'He's with me,' she said quietly. They
walked up to the stable, where another
police officer was guarding something
on the floor. Rose was called in by the
police when there was a supernatural
killing. John was writing a book on
vampires and this was good research.

Logan gasped when he saw the body.
There was a wooden stake in its chest.
'Look at his face. How old did you say

he was?' said John

'The years catch up with vampires when they die. Paul was about two hundred years old,' Rose explained. 'He was at the club last night with his girlfriend. Tara nearly died here too.'

'But why come out of Brighton to this stable?' asked John.

'I think the killer was putting on a show. He or she must have used the white stallion test. Horses can identify vampires. Paul didn't stand a chance. Luckily for Tara, she was able to escape and ride the horse to safety.'

Logan turned away. He felt very angry. 'We must catch whoever did this before they strike again.'

'Paul was a popular guy,' said Rose

Petal. She looked worried. 'As soon as word gets out about the way he died, Brighton's vampires will be angry and afraid. Some will want revenge.'

'The police won't want vampire attacks to happen in the city,' said John. 'Whoever this vampire hater is, we need to act fast.'

****

That evening, Lomax rang the door of a neat little house in the Kemp Town district of Brighton.

'Hello. Are you Edward James, the maths tutor?' he said.

'Yes, that's me,' said Edward. 'You must be Lomax. You're right on time. Come in.'

Edward James was dressed in black. He only looked about twenty but he had yellow teeth and very pale skin.

'Have we met before?' he said to Lomax. 'You were at Vampires Inc. last night, weren't you?'

Lomax stared at him. 'Are you saying I'm a vampire?'

'No, I just ...'

'I'm not a vampire, but you are,' said Lomax, pushing Edward against the wall. 'And it seems my maths is better than I thought. You're number two on my list.'

'I think you should leave,' said Edward. His voice was quiet but his fangs were starting to show. Lomax went to the front door and let in his friends. They were all carrying crosses, which they held out in front of them. Edward stepped back and Lomax laughed.

'Give me your phone, bloodsucker,' said Lomax. Edward handed over his phone and watched as Lomax scanned through the contacts list.

'All the names of Brighton's undead are in here,' said Lomax. 'We'll kill them, one by one, until Brighton is clean again.'

The gang held their crosses in Edward's face and he backed away.

'You won't get away with this. Rose Petal will stop you. She keeps us safe. You'll see,' shouted Edward as the gang pushed him to the floor.

'Then we'll make sure to pay this Rose Petal a visit too. Thanks for the tip,' said Lomax. 'Now, it's time to forget about maths — you're history!'

****

Logan called up the stairs of Vampires Inc. to Rose's flat. 'So what have you found out?' he asked.

'It was the group who were in the club last night. The leader is called Lomax. Apparently Paul and Tara left with them to go to a party. I've asked questions everywhere. Nobody knows who they are or where they came from,' she replied.

Just then, Rose's phone rang. She spoke quickly, then hung up and grabbed her bag. 'There's been another vampire murder,' she said. 'Let's go.'

The little house where Edward James had been found was in a quiet side street. John and Rose walked through the house and into the garden.

'He was buried upside down, with garlic in his mouth,' said the police officer who had called Rose.

'That's a common way of dealing with a vampire, if you believe in old folk tales about them rising again,' Rose replied.

Logan turned away. 'These people are sick,' he said.

Rose took photos of the body. 'Edward James used to come to the club a lot,' she said. 'He liked to hang around with the human crowd. He just found them friendly and fun.'

'Well, there's nothing friendly or fun about this gang,' said John. 'Are there any clues from inside the house?'

They went into the house. The police officer had found a power lead for a mobile phone, but no handset. While they were searching the house, Rose quickly checked Edward's laptop. It was connected to the data from the mobile phone and she printed off a list of his contacts.

'The killers might use Edward's phone to contact other vampires in Brighton. Let's ring everyone on this list and tell them to be careful,' said Rose Petal. 'Nobody's safe now.'

Chapter 3

It was late in the evening. Rose Petal
was going to bed when there was a
knock on the door of her flat. Rose
turned out the lights and let Danny, her
white owl, out of his cage. He looked at
her with his big green eyes. She knew
whose side he was on.

'Who is it?' she asked through the
door.

'I'm a friend of Edward James. He
told me you helped keep vampires
safe,' said a male voice.

Rose opened the door. Lomax and
his friends pushed in.

'Hold the vampire lover,' sneered Lomax. 'She runs the club where all those freaks get together.' He turned to his friends. 'If she wants to be a vampire, we should treat her like one. A stake through the heart should do it.'

'You'll never get away with this,' she shouted at them.

'If you're not here anymore, the club and shop will have to shut down. The vampires will go somewhere else and we'll be half way to cleaning up Brighton,' laughed the woman in Lomax's gang.

'My boyfriend is here. You wouldn't want to meet him,' said Rose, angrily.

'That's good. Now we can kill both of you!' said Lomax.

With a flap of his strong wings, Danny came at the vampire haters. He saw even better in the dark. He dived at them with his sharp claws. Screeching and whirling, he pecked and scratched at the gang. They headed for the door with their arms over their eyes. Rose heard them run down the street, then they were gone. For now.

Rose shut the door and bolted it. Her hands were shaking as she found her phone.

'John, please come over now,' she said. 'Lomax just tried to kill me.'

****

When he got there, John put his arm round Rose.

'Danny saved my life,' she sobbed. 'There were four of them, I couldn't fight them off on my own.'

'I hate to ask when you're so upset, but can you think of anything that might help us to track them down?' said John.

'I should be able to identify Lomax now I've seen him close up,' said Rose, wiping her eyes. 'We can log onto the police's criminal database to find out more.'

Rose and John settled at Rose's laptop and started to look at records for criminals called Lomax. Before long, Rose gasped. 'That's him!'

'We must catch them before they strike

Name:

LOMAX FENTON

Criminal history:

Race hatred, murder

Current status:

Escaped from

Winlaw Prison,

Scotland

Notes:

Lomax Fenton has become obsessed

with vampires while in prison.

Fenton accused another inmate of being

a vampire and killed him in his cell.

His girlfriend, also a convicted murderer,

helped him to escape last week.

again,' said Rose. 'They'll be using Edward James's contacts to choose their next victim.'

Just then, a blinding pain shot through John's head. He squeezed his eyes shut as he heard Rodney's voice. It was as if Rose's friend, the half werewolf, was standing next to him. This had happened before.

'John, help me. Find Rose. Paul's killers have got me. Come to Beachy Head. Quickly!'

John told Rose who didn't waste any time. She called a number that she didn't ever think she would need to ring. 'Is that you, Rob?' she said, when a man answered. 'It's Rose Petal. We need your help.'

Rob Robson was the leader of the Lukos Chapter. They were a gang of bikers who were also werewolves. They didn't like the vampires in Brighton, and often fought them. But this was different – the gang had one of their own kind. Rodney was half werewolf – they had to help Rose save him.

Chapter 4

Within minutes, Rob's biker gang was outside Vampires Inc., revving their motors

'I hope you know what you're doing, Rose,' said John, as they pulled on their crash helmets. John climbed onto the back of one of the motorbikes. Rose jumped on behind Rob Robson. He closed his visor and nodded. With another roar of their engines, the Lukos Chapter set off for Eastbourne. Their speed took John's breath away. The bikes were like wild beasts let loose. Soon, they arrived at the cliff.

Beachy Head was well known for being somewhere that people killed themselves by jumping from the cliff into the sea. Rodney was standing on the very edge of the cliff with Lomax's vampire-hating gang.

The thick hairs on Rodney's arms were standing on end. John knew he could read minds as well as speak to people through their thoughts. Suddenly Rodney spoke in a low voice.

'I see a vampire that hates himself. I see a vampire who has to face up to what he really is before he dies forever.'

'Shut up!' shouted Lomax. 'You're the one who's going to die here!' He pointed to the waves lashing the rocks at the bottom of the cliff.

'Let him go!' cried Rose.

John heard a roar behind him and looked back. Rob's gang had transformed into their full werewolf selves. He looked up at the night sky — it was a full moon. The werewolves would be at their most dangerous.

'Hey Lomax, look up,' yelled John. As Lomax glanced up to the sky, Rodney twisted free from him and ran to safety behind the bikers. With a snarl, Rob began to lead his gang around Rose, John and Rodney. They padded silently towards Lomax. The gang look at each other nervously. 'Do something,' hissed the woman. 'I didn't get you out of prison to die here!'

Lomax put his head down. Then he lifted it slowly, with an evil smile on his face. In the moonlight, his eyes glowed red and his fangs glittered. Lomax was a vampire. 'Look at what I have become!' he hissed.

Lomax flew at Rob Robson. The werewolf raised itself on its back legs and leapt through the air at the vampire. They crashed to the ground and became a blur of sharp teeth, claws and fur. Lomax tried to pin down the werewolf, while the other members of the Lukos Chapter circled around the rest of his gang. Lomax's girlfriend started to run away. The wind caught her scream as she slipped off the edge of the cliff.

Lomax paused at the sound of his girlfriend's last cry. In that moment, Rob sunk his teeth into the vampire's throat. It was all over.

Chapter 5

The next day, John and Rose were back at Vampires Inc., talking about what happened. 'So Lomax was a vampire,' said John. 'I really did not see that coming.'

'Somebody in prison must have made him one,' replied Rose. 'No wonder he was so full of hate.' She clicked away on her laptop. 'Hmm. This is interesting. You know his girlfriend was in prison too? It turns out she killed her father ...'

'... because she thought he was a vampire,' John finished the sentence.

'What will the werewolves do with the rest of Lomax's gang?'

'They're going to take them back to prison and probably give them a few frights on the way. At least the vampires of Brighton are safe again,' said Rose.

'This is also good for my book,' said John. 'Everything that has happened over the last day or so has given me some great ideas. It was so cool when Rodney read Lomax's mind and told him to face his true self.'

'When people read your book, they'll think you made everything up,' said Rose. 'Only we will know it all really happened.'

'You've shown me some amazing

things,' said John. 'But can I ask you one more favour?'

'I guess so,' replied Rose.

'Could you please ask Rodney to stop getting inside my head? It really freaks me out!'

Rose laughed. 'I'll take care of it.'

'Thanks Rose, I know you will,' smiled John. 'You seem to take care of everything.' John knew that with Rose on his side, he could face anything too.

Glossary

criminal database – a list of all the criminals in the country

garlic – a herb used in cooking which vampires cannot stand

Halloween – the night of the year, on 31 October, when people dress up as witches and ghosts

inmate – a person who is in prison

obsessed – when a person holds an interest and cannot stop thinking about it day or night

race hatred – hating others who have a different skin colour and seeking to bully and attack them

transformed – when the shape of your body has changed and become something different

Quiz

1 Why is there a big party at Vampires Inc.?

2 What does Lomax look like?

3 How does the white stallion test work?

4 Why does Lomax go to see the maths tutor, Edward James?

5 What does Lomax take away from Edward James's house?

6 Who saves Rose Petal's life?

7 How does Rodney tell Rose that he is being held prisoner?

8 What is the name of the werewolf gang?

9 What transport do they use?

10 What happened to Lomax while he was in prison?

Quiz answers

1 It is Halloween

2 He is tall with blond hair

3 White horses can identify vampires — they get very scared when they smell a vampire

4 He knows he is a vampire and he wants to kill him

5 A mobile phone with the contacts of many more vampires

6 Danny, her white owl

7 He speaks through John Logan's mind

8 The Lukos Chapter

9 Motorbikes

10 He was bitten by a vampire and became one

About the author

The author of these books teaches in a London school. At the weekend, his research takes him to the beaches and back streets of Brighton in search of werewolves and vampires.

He writes about what he has found.